# Matilda Mae
## Wears Confidence

Susan Howard

Illustration by Mike Coller

Copyright © 2022 by Susan Howard

All rights reserved. No part of this book may be reproduced or transmitted in any form or by any means, electronic or mechanical, including photocopying, recording, or by any information storage and retrieval system, without permission in writing from the publisher. For information regarding permission, contact the publisher.

Dedicated to –

My children
Aiden, Grayson, and Winter
My strength and motivation
To my parents
Vic and Grace (Chela)
My infinite support and love

My name is Matilda Mae, but my friends call me Mattie. Tomorrow is my first day in a new school, but I'm a little scared. My hands are sweaty, and I have knots in my tummy that will not go away. I can't even eat dinner, and it's pepperoni pizza with extra cheese, my favorite!

"Don't worry, Matilda Mae. Your new school will be fun," Mom says.
But I'm not so sure.
"You're gonna make so many new friends. You're going to have a great time," Dad says. But I'm not so sure.

Mom stands up to clear the table of my pizza slice with only one bite out of it. She places the dishes in the sink. Dad gets up to throw away the pizza box, and I sulk in my chair a little more.

"It'll be okay, sweetheart," Mom says as she bends down and runs a finger through my hair.

I look down at my arm and see my birthmark. Mom always said it looked like a pink heart, but I just think it looks like a giant red splotch, as if someone splashed strawberry jam on me, only it won't wash off. Now I'm worried. What if the kids in my class think I have jam all over my arm?

Mom and Dad tuck me into bed. They tell me to have sweet dreams, but my dreams are not sweet at all. I dream that my new school is so tall that it reaches up to the sky. There are no new friends and no nice teachers. It's just a cold, gray empty building. My eyes pop open, and I can barely catch my breath. I squeeze my stuffed unicorn. It takes me a long time before I am able to fall back asleep.

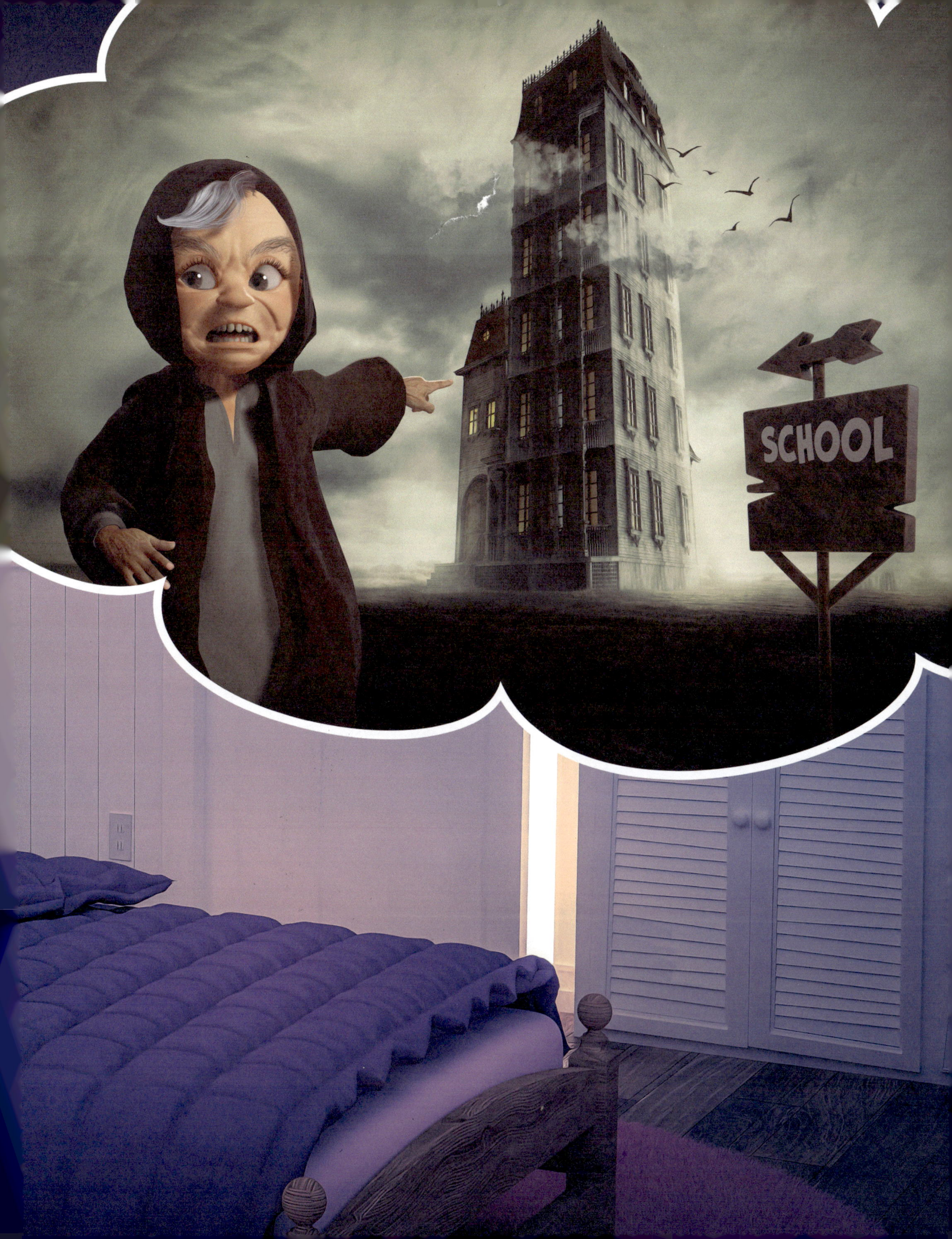
SCHOOL

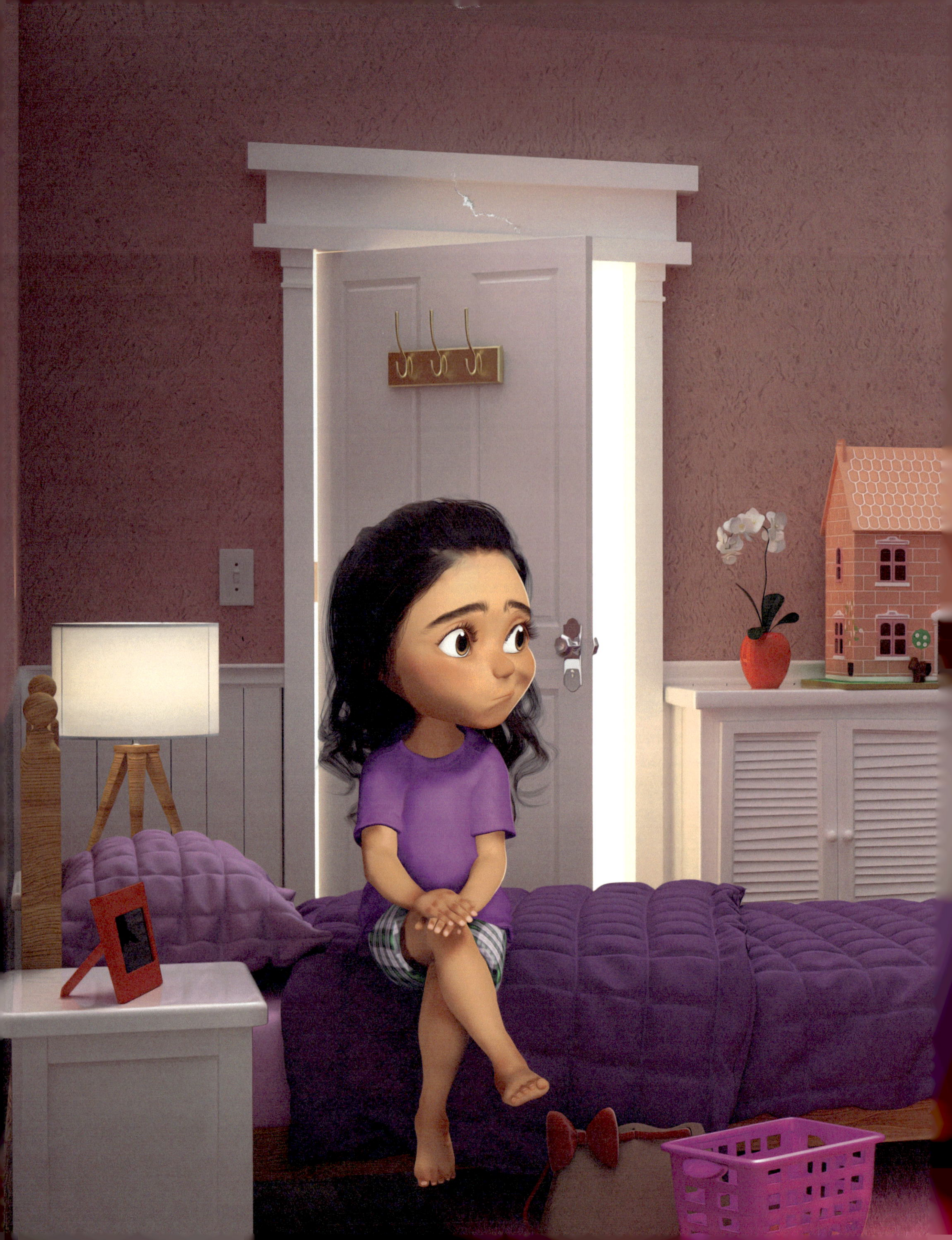

In the morning, I don't feel any better, but I still brush my teeth and wash my face. Mom walks into my room holding the new purple dress she bought for my first day. I remembered seeing it in the store window when we went shopping. I scrunch my nose. Yesterday I thought it was so beautiful, but now I'm not so sure. It has pretty pink flowers scattered all over the fabric, and it's soft when I run my fingers across it. But now that I look closer, the sleeves are too short. Way too short to cover my blob of a birthmark.

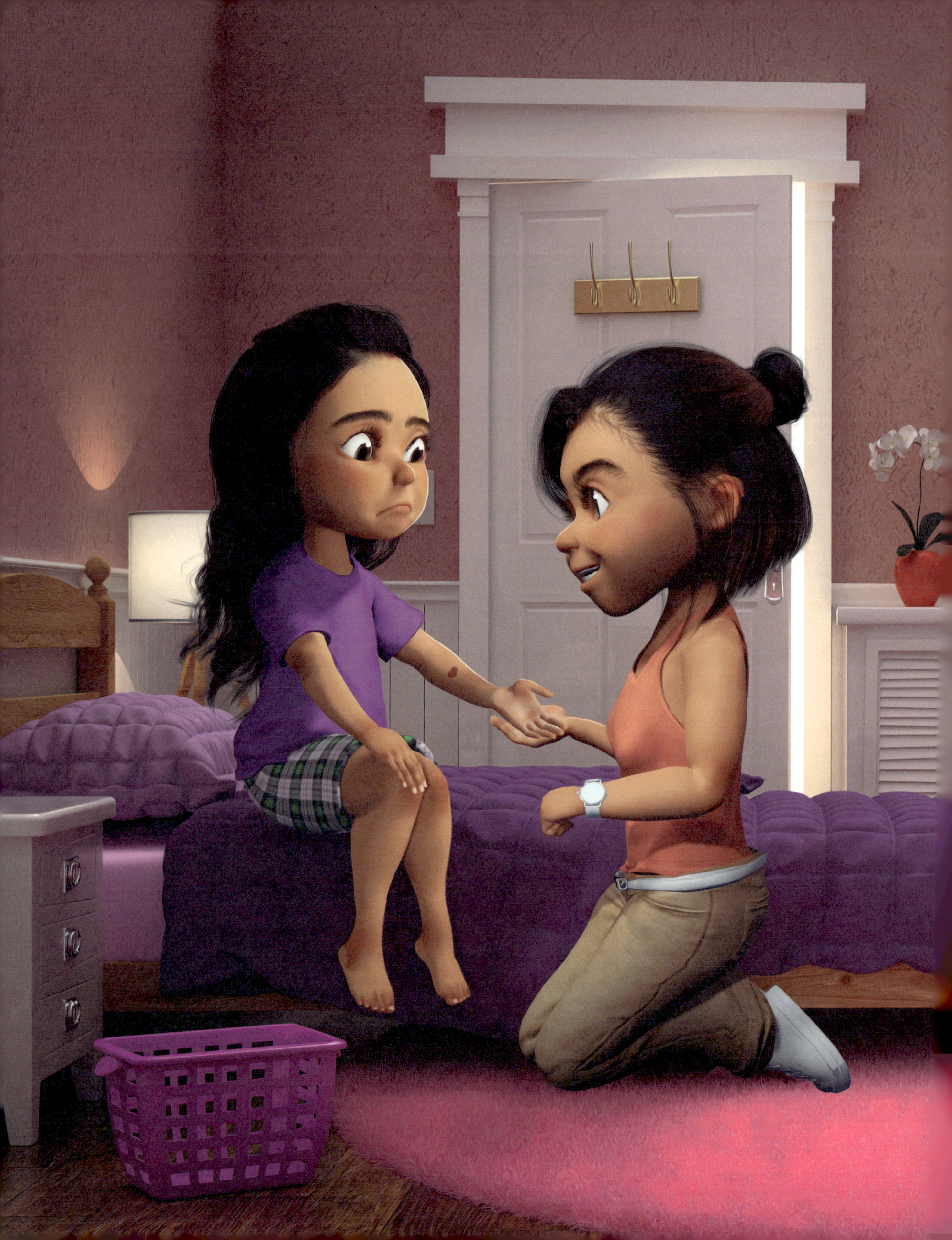

I look down, and it's staring right back at me. I cover it with my hand. I beg Mom to let me cover it with a bandage. Instead, she kneels next to me, takes my hand, and gives it a little kiss.

"Every part of you is beautiful, Matilda Mae, every single part. In fact, I don't think this is a birthmark. I think this is a beauty mark." She smiles. She gives me a squeeze and tells me it's time to go.

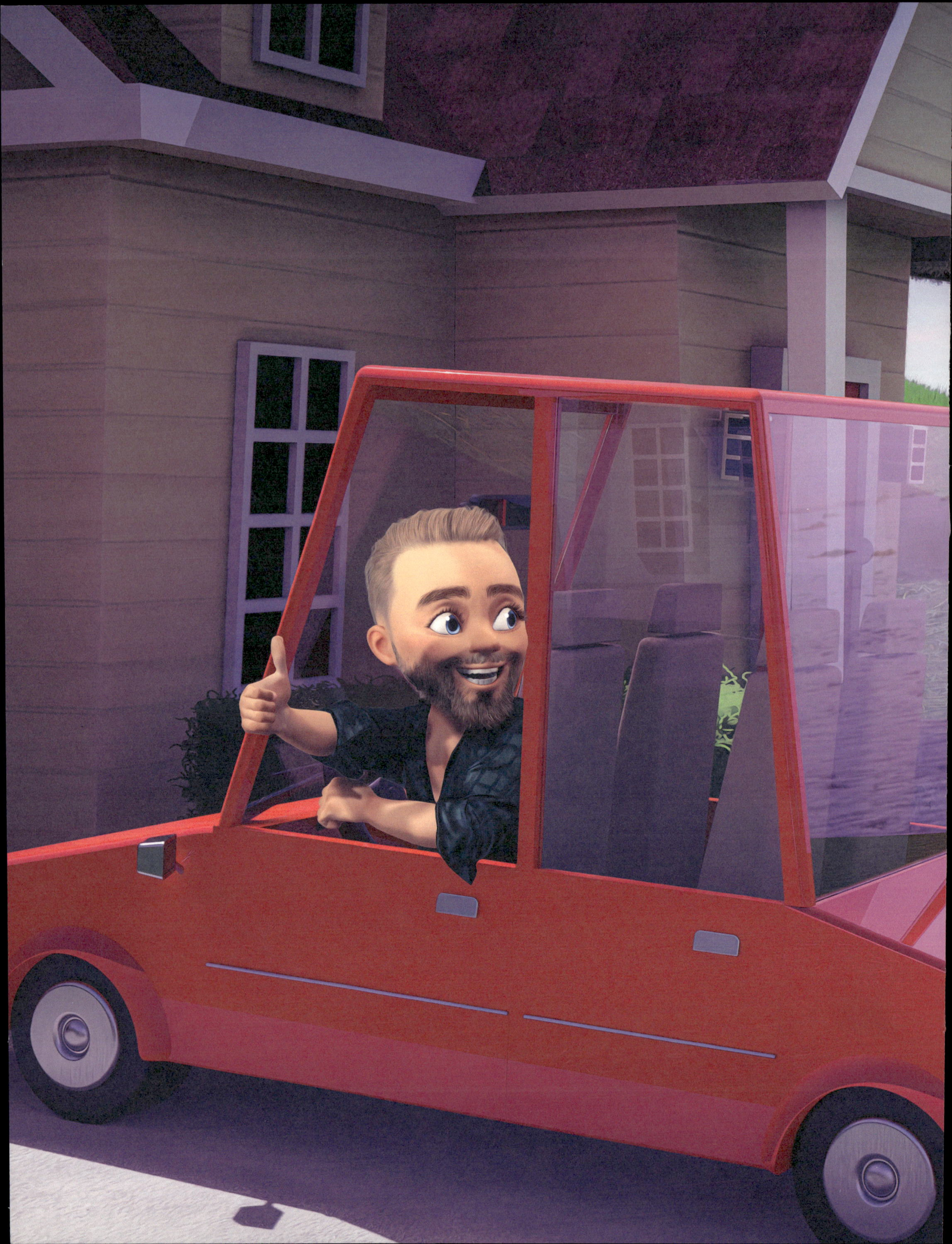

Dad is waiting in the car. He gives me a thumbs up and says today is going to be a great day. I'm still not so sure. Mom buckles up in the seat next to Dad while I slide into my seat and stare at my feet.

I feel a little better when we pull up to the school. It isn't as big as I imagined. It's just right.

Mom walks me to my new classroom. There are so many kids. A few girls are standing at one end of the room talking together. A red-headed boy is showing another boy his light-up yo-yo. The teacher smiles as I stand near the door, too nervous to move.

900-930 Language Arts Language Arts Language Arts
930-1005 PE PE PE
1005-1040 Language Arts Language Arts Language Arts
1040-1110 Lunch Lunch & Recess Lunch
1110-1210 Math Math Math
1210-110 Science Science Science
110-140 Social Studies Social Studies Social Studies
140-200 Recess- Upper Recess-
200-225 Music Computer Art
Pack Up Pack Up Pack Up
Healthcare Infographic

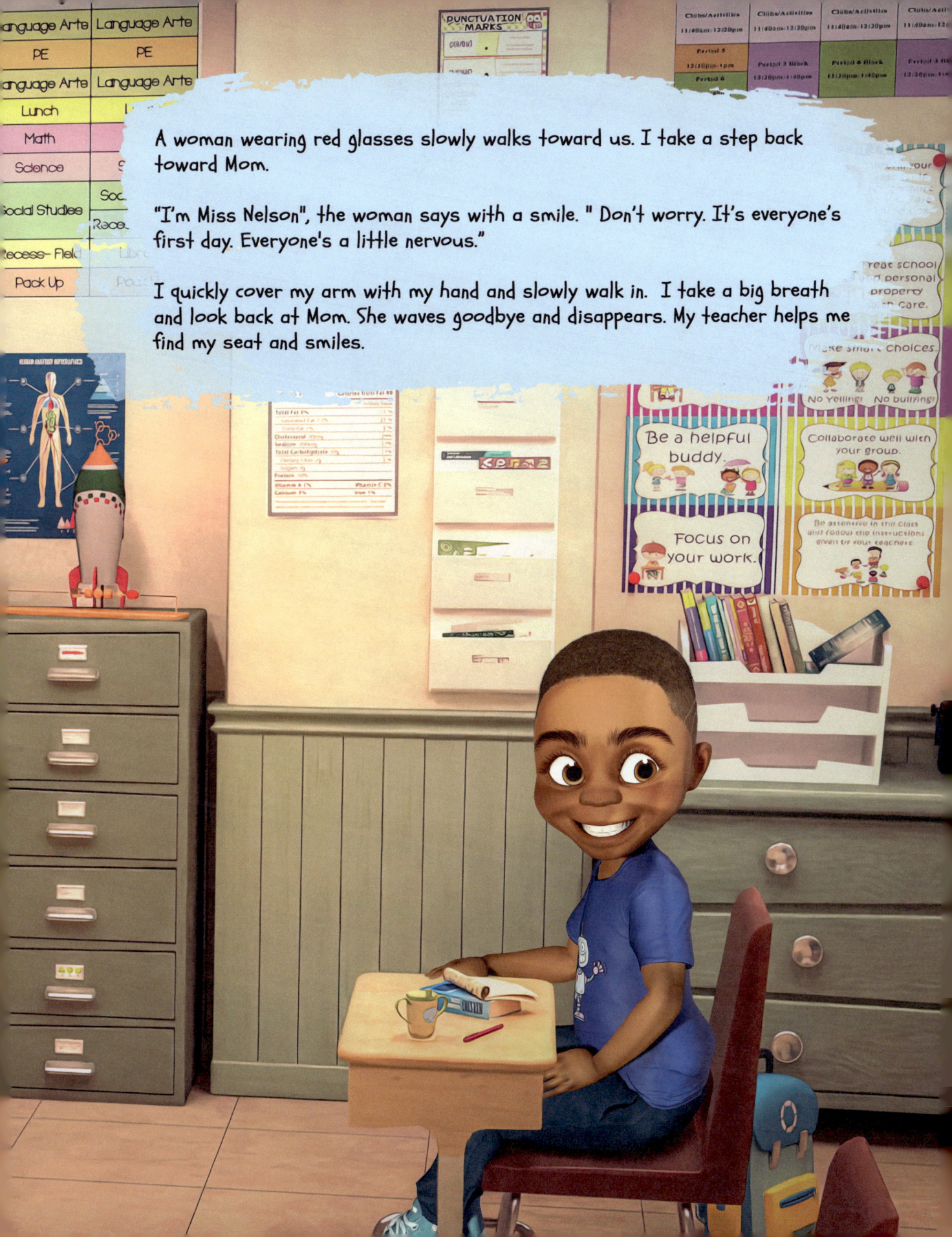

A woman wearing red glasses slowly walks toward us. I take a step back toward Mom.

"I'm Miss Nelson", the woman says with a smile. " Don't worry. It's everyone's first day. Everyone's a little nervous."

I quickly cover my arm with my hand and slowly walk in. I take a big breath and look back at Mom. She waves goodbye and disappears. My teacher helps me find my seat and smiles.

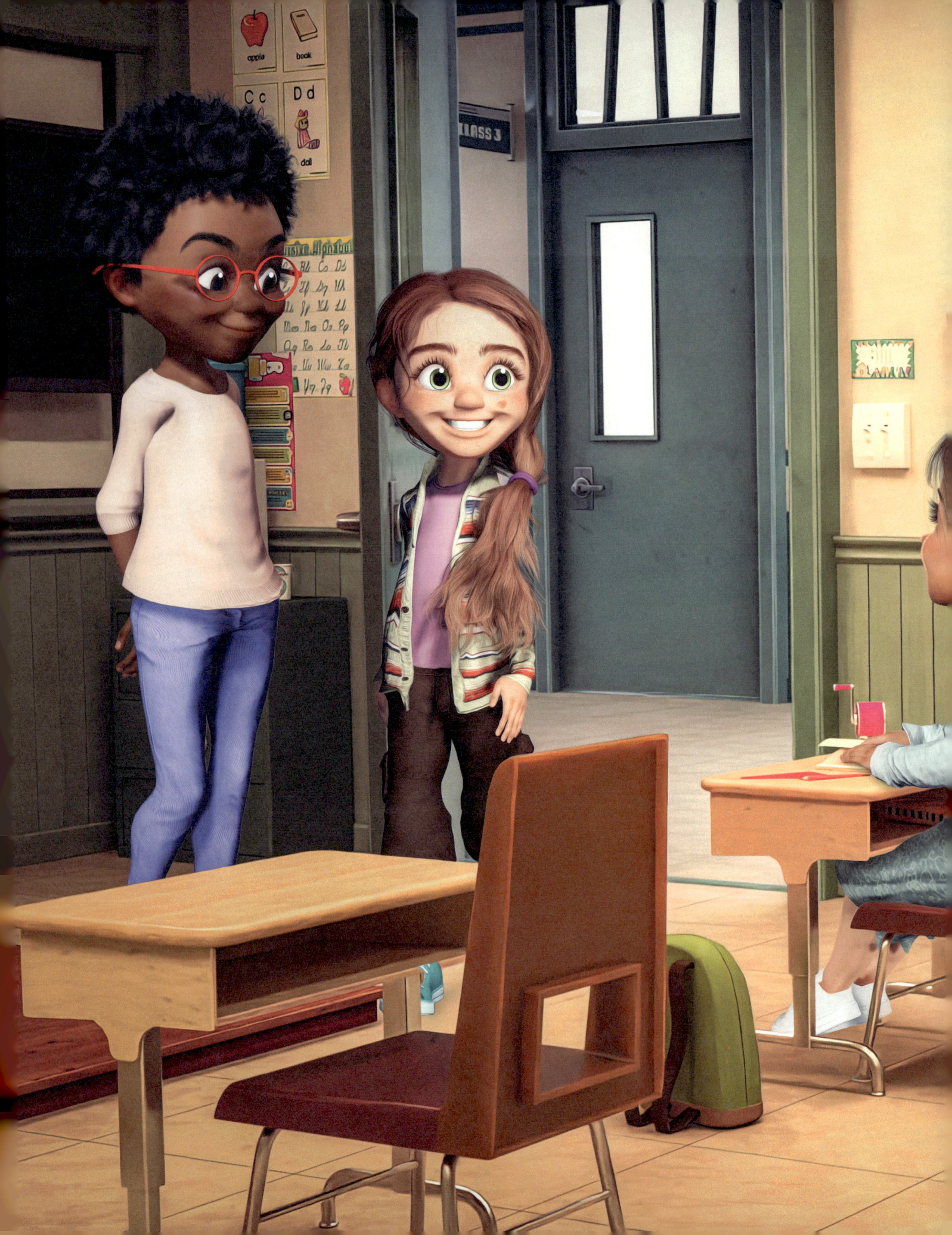

apple
book
C c
D d
doll

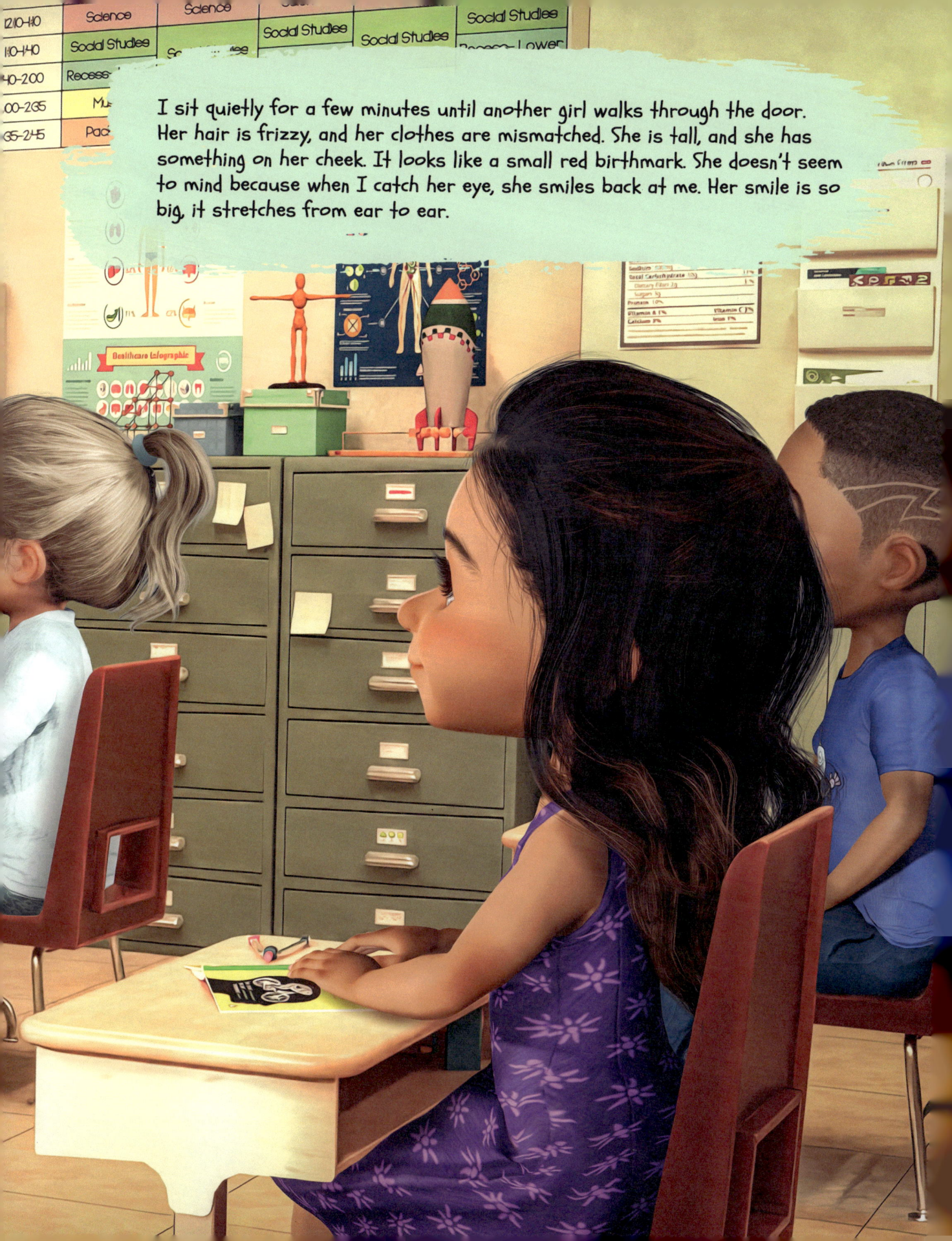

I sit quietly for a few minutes until another girl walks through the door. Her hair is frizzy, and her clothes are mismatched. She is tall, and she has something on her cheek. It looks like a small red birthmark. She doesn't seem to mind because when I catch her eye, she smiles back at me. Her smile is so big, it stretches from ear to ear.

"Hello, everyone! Grace is here. The party can begin!" she bellows. She walks straight to the empty seat in front of me and plops down.

All the kids stare at her. I can tell they are all wondering who she is. I am wondering too.

Why doesn't she seem to care about her birthmark?

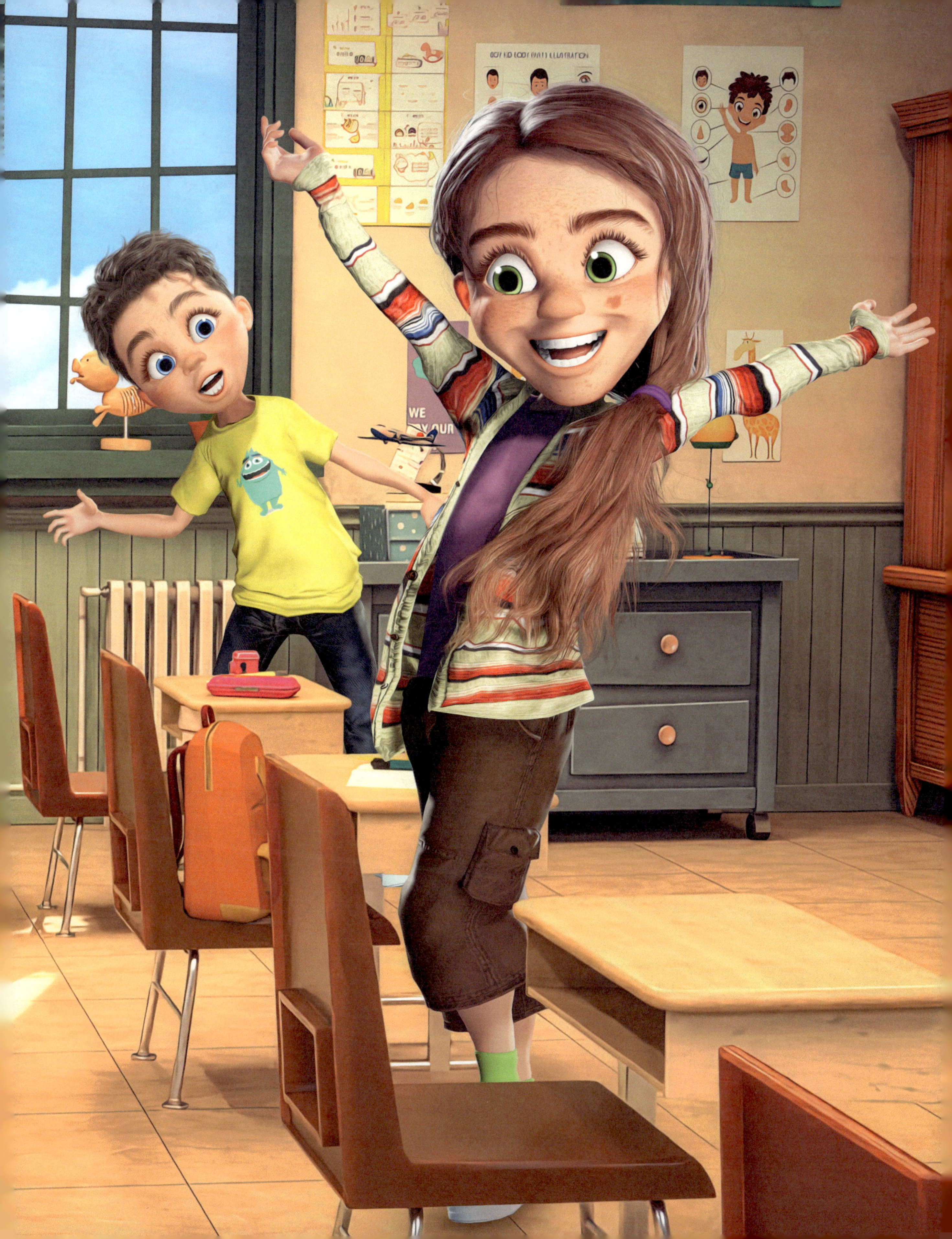
WE

For the rest of the day, Grace keeps her smile planted on her face. She doesn't even seem to notice the two girls whispering or pointing at her. She doesn't see the boy next to me lean so far over his desk to get a closer look at her that he almost falls off his chair

The rest of the day, I stare at Grace, who seems to enjoy every bit of the school day. Oh, how I wish I could be as confident as she is.

WE RESPECT EACH OTHER.
WE CELEBRATE EACH OTHER'S SUCCESS.
WE ARE A TEAM.
WE CREATE
WE TRY OUR BEST.
WE LEARN FROM MISTAKES.

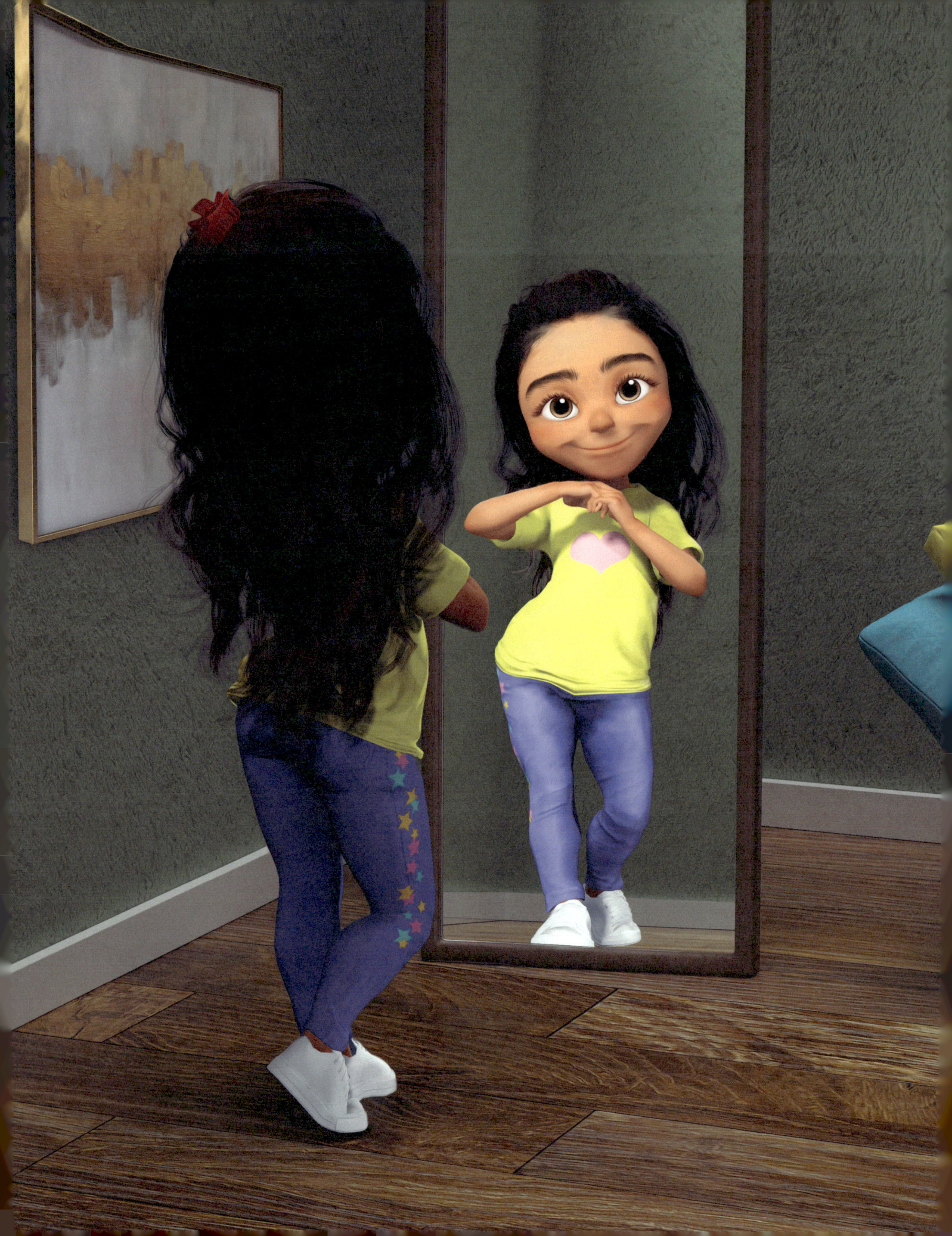

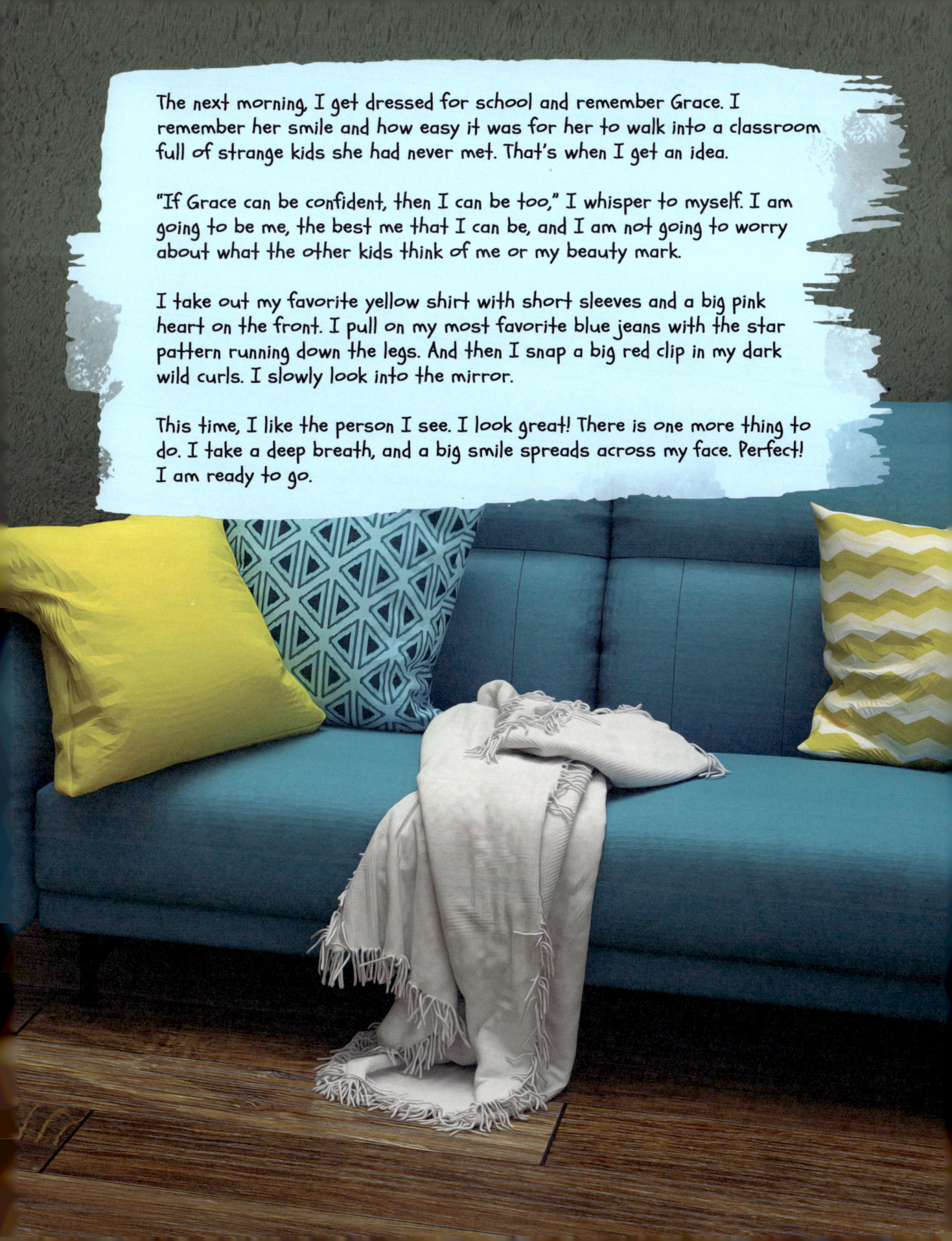

The next morning, I get dressed for school and remember Grace. I remember her smile and how easy it was for her to walk into a classroom full of strange kids she had never met. That's when I get an idea.

"If Grace can be confident, then I can be too," I whisper to myself. I am going to be me, the best me that I can be, and I am not going to worry about what the other kids think of me or my beauty mark.

I take out my favorite yellow shirt with short sleeves and a big pink heart on the front. I pull on my most favorite blue jeans with the star pattern running down the legs. And then I snap a big red clip in my dark wild curls. I slowly look into the mirror.

This time, I like the person I see. I look great! There is one more thing to do. I take a deep breath, and a big smile spreads across my face. Perfect! I am ready to go.

Mom is waiting for me by the door. She hands me my bookbag and my lunch. Dad is already in the car.

"Today is going to be a great day, Matilda Mae," he says.

This time, I give him a thumbs up.

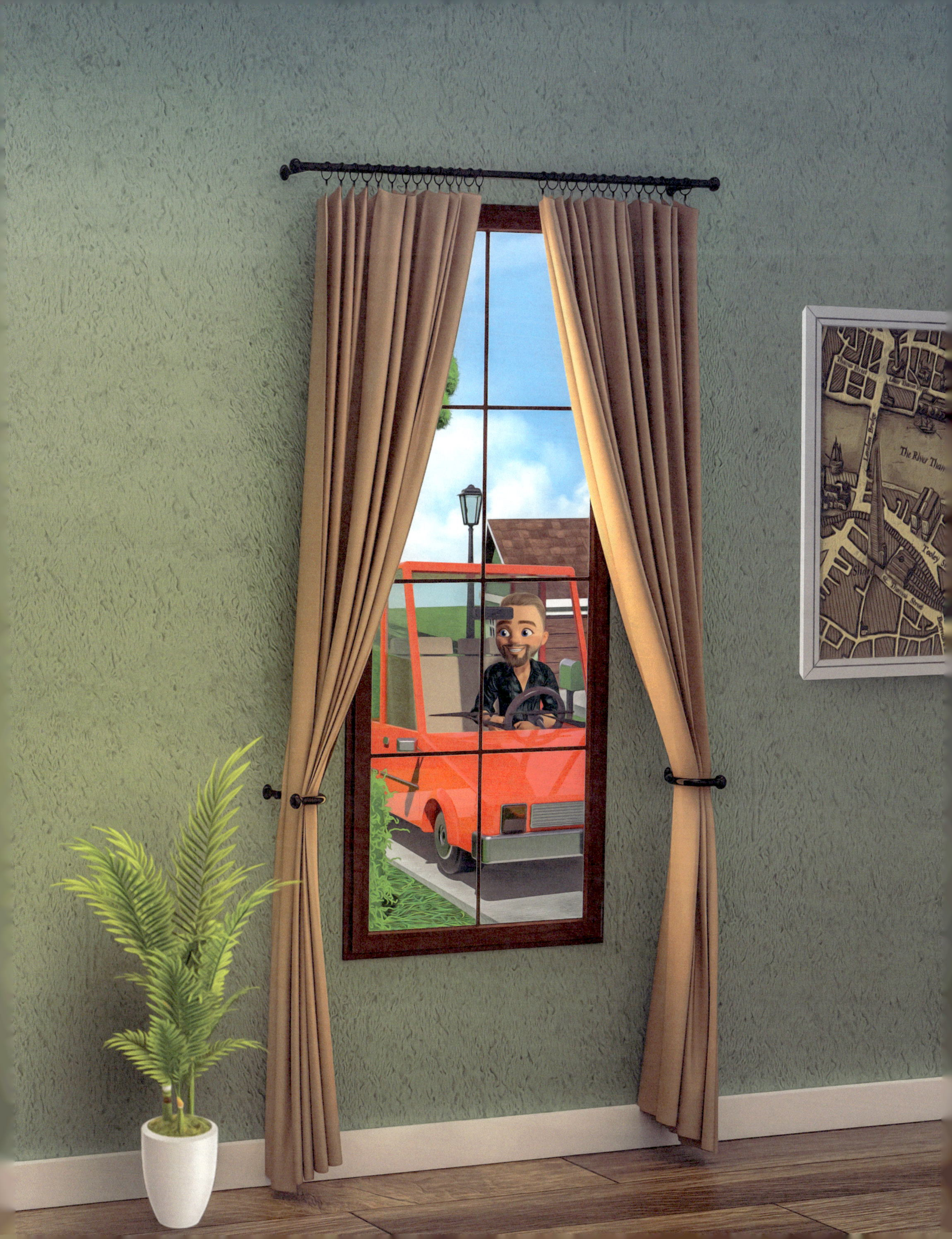

Thames Street
The River Tham
Tooley S

When we arrive at school, I take a deep breath. "I can go in by myself today," I say to Mom. I give her a hug goodbye and walk into school. I stand in front of the big door to my classroom for a moment before turning the knob and opening the door.

Grace is sitting in her seat. Some of the other kids are crowded around her. They are smiling too. I hold my chin up and walk straight to my chair. I take my seat. Grace turns around, tossing her frizzy hair over one shoulder.

"Hi," she says "I'm Grace. I like your shirt."

"Hi," I say back with a large, toothy grin. "I'm Matilda Mae, but you can call me Mattie."

Check out book 2: "Matilda Mae Is Green With Envy"

## About the Author:

As a former educator, Susan Howard continues to teach children life lessons through her writing. She was born in Chicago, Illinois. She now lives in Beaumont, Texas with her husband and three children. When she's not playing with her children, she is reading, relaxing outdoors, and of course...writing.

Made in the USA
Columbia, SC
30 October 2024